ABOUT THE BANK STREET READY-TO-READ SERIES

Seventy years of educational research and innovative teaching have given the Bank Street College of Education the reputation as America's most trusted name in early childhood education.

Because no two children are exactly alike in their development, we have designed the *Bank Street Ready-to-Read* series in three levels to accommodate the individual stages of reading readiness of children ages four through eight.

- ◉ *Level 1:* GETTING READY TO READ—read-alouds for children who are taking their first steps toward reading.
- ◉ *Level 2:* READING TOGETHER—for children who are just beginning to read by themselves but may need a little help.
- ○ *Level 3:* I CAN READ IT MYSELF—for children who can read independently.

Our three levels make it easy to select the books most appropriate for a child's development and enable him or her to grow with the series step by step. The *Bank Street Ready-to-Read* books also overlap and reinforce each other, further encouraging the reading process.

We feel that making reading fun and enjoyable is the single most important thing that you can do to help children become good readers. And we hope you'll be a part of Bank Street's long tradition of learning through sharing.

The Bank Street College of Education

To Delroy Drumgold
— B.B.
To Emily
— J.E.C.

TOO MANY MICE

A Bantam Little Rooster Book/August 1992

Little Rooster is a trademark of Bantam Books,
a division of Bantam Doubleday Dell Publishing Group, Inc.

Series graphic design by Alex Jay/Studio J

Special thanks to James A. Levine, Betsy Gould,
Diane Arico, and Evelyne Johnson.

Library of Congress Cataloging-in-Publication Data

Brenner, Barbara.
Too many mice/by Barbara Brenner;
illustrated by John Emil Cymerman.
p. cm. — (Bank Street ready-to-read)
"A Byron Preiss book."
"A Bantam little rooster book."
Summary: When Nita and her mother use
a bunch of cats to get rid of the mice
in their house, it is only the beginning
of a proliferation of animals.
ISBN 0-553-07757-O. — ISBN 0-553-35160-5 (pbk.)
[1. Animals — Fiction. I. Cymerman, John Emil, ill.
II. Title. III. Series.
PZ7.B7518To 1992
[E] — dc20
91-29687 CIP AC

Published simultaneously in the United States and Canada

Bantam Books are published by Bantam Books, a division of Bantam Doubleday Dell
Publishing Group, Inc. Its trademark, consisting of the words "Bantam Books" and the
portrayal of a rooster, is Registered in U.S. Patent and Trademark Office and in other
countries. Marca Registrada. Bantam Books, 666 Fifth Avenue, New York, New York 10103.

PRINTED IN THE UNITED STATES OF AMERICA

0 9 8 7 6 5 4 3

Bank Street Ready-to-Read™

Too Many Mice

by Barbara Brenner
Illustrated by
John Emil Cymerman

A Byron Preiss Book

A BANTAM LITTLE ROOSTER BOOK

NEW YORK · TORONTO · LONDON · SYDNEY · AUCKLAND

Nita and her mama
lived in a house
with one cat.
There was one cat,
but there were *many* mice.
Too many.

There were mice in the bedroom.
There were mice on the stairs.

6

There were mice in the kitchen
and mice under chairs.
There were too many mice
for one cat to catch.

"There are too many mice
in this house," said Mama.
"We need more cats."
"You are right, Mama,"
said Nita.
So Nita went looking for cats.

She ran up and down the street,
calling cats.
"Here kitty, kitty.
I know where you can find
a nice mouse dinner."

The cats came running.
A white cat,
a striped cat,

a cat with a crooked tail,
a cat with shining eyes,
and a mama cat with kittens.

The cats ran into Nita's house,
and soon all the mice ran out.

"That's better," said Mama.
"Now I will sit down
and read my paper."

But she couldn't sit down.
There was a cat in Mama's chair.
There were cats everywhere!

Nita's mama sighed.
"Now there are too many cats."
"You are right, Mama," said Nita.
"We need dogs to chase the cats."

Nita ran up and down the street.
"Here dogs, here dogs,"
she called.
"I know where you can find
lots of cats to chase."

The dogs
came running.
A black dog,
a white dog,
a big dog,
a small dog,
and a dog
with spots.
The dogs went
into the house,
and the cats
ran out!

"Now I can sit down and
read my paper," said Mama.
But she couldn't sit down.
A dog was in Mama's chair.
There were dogs everywhere!

"We have too many dogs,"
said Mama.
"You are right, Mama,"
said Nita.
"We need some alligators
to scare the dogs."

Nita went to the alligator pond.
"Alli, alli, gator," she called.
"I know where you can scare
some dogs!"
Two alligators popped up.

They crawled out of the pond,
down the street,
and into the house.
Snap! Snap! went their big teeth.
All the dogs ran away!

24

"Maybe now I can read my paper,"
said Mama.
But just then,
Snap! Snap!
An alligator ate Mama's paper.
"Alligators are worse than dogs!"
cried Mama.
"Mama, you are right,"
said Nita.
"We need an elephant
to scare the alligators."

Nita went to the zoo.
She rented an elephant.
The elephant walked into the house.
Thump! Thump!
It shook the whole house.

The alligators were scared.
They crawled down the stairs
and back to their pond.

"Now that's better,"
said Mama.
"Let's go to bed."

Nita and Mama lay down.
But the elephant stayed up.
Thump! Thump! Thump!
Beds shook, chairs broke,
and dishes came crashing down.

"This will not do," said Mama.
"Even one elephant is too many."
"You are right, Mama," said Nita.

"But there's only one thing
that will scare an elephant."
"What is that?" asked Mama.

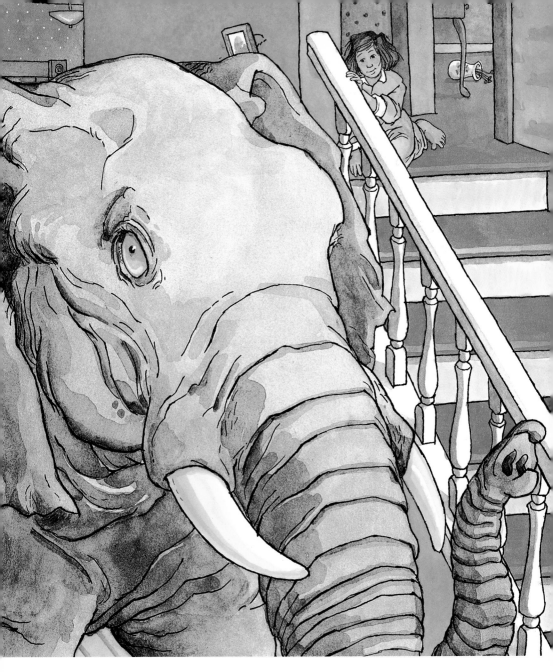

"A mouse!" said Nita.